Good Night, Monkey Boy

GOOD NIGHT, MONKEY BOY

Jarrett J. Krosoczka

Dragonfly Books —— New York

Copyright © 2001 by Jarrett J. Krosoczka

All rights reserved. Published in the United States by Dragonfly Books,
an imprint of Random House Children's Books, a division of Random House, Inc., New York.
Originally published in hardcover in the United States by Alfred A. Knopf,
an imprint of Random House Children's Books, a division of Random House, Inc., New York, in 2001.

Dragonfly Books with the colophon is a registered trademark of Random House, Inc.

Visit us on the Web! www.randomhouse.com/kids

Educators and librarians, for a variety of teaching tools, visit us at
www.randomhouse.com/teachers

Library of Congress Cataloging-in-Publication Data
Krosoczka, Jarrett.
Good Night, Monkey Boy / Jarrett J. Krosoczka.
p. cm.
Summary: A mother tries to get her mischievous son, whom she calls Monkey Boy, to bed.
ISBN 978-0-375-81121-0 (trade) — ISBN 978-0-375-91121-7 (lib. bdg.) — ISBN 978-0-440-41798-9 (pbk.)
[1. Bedtime—Fiction. 2. Mothers and sons—Fiction.] I. Title.
PZ7.K935 Go 2001 [E]—dc21 00059922

MANUFACTURED IN CHINA

12 11 10 9 8 7 6 5

For Grandma and Grandpa,
the best parents a kid could ask for

"My, look at the time."

"Let's get ready
for bed,
Monkey Boy."

"Sorry, no bananas before bedtime, Monkey Boy."

"Now let's brush your teeth."

"Enough of that!"

"Bath time,
Monkey Boy."

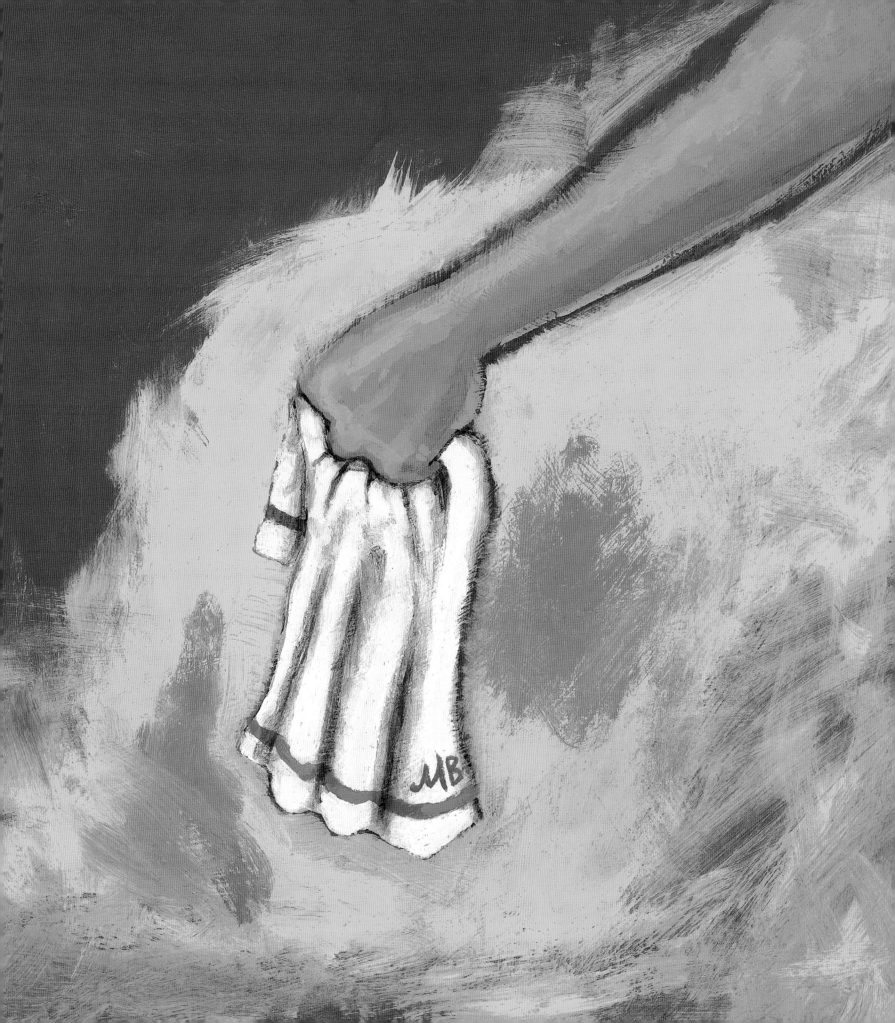

"Monkey Boy, get down from there!"

"Of course
I'll read
you a story..."

"...after you put these toys away!"

"Come along now—
I'll tuck you in."

"Once there
was a
monkey..."

"I said no bananas!"

"Good night, Monkey Boy."

"I love you, too, Monkey Boy."

"Go to sleep,
Monkey Boy!"